Let's Learn
Aesop's Fables

The Town Mouse
and the
Country Mouse

WINDMILL
BOOKS

Published in 2018 by Windmill Books, an Imprint of Rosen Publishing | 29 East 21st Street, New York, NY 10010
Copyright © 2018 Windmill Books | All rights reserved. No part of this book may be reproduced in any
form without permission in writing from the publisher, except by a reviewer. | Illustrator: Andy Rowland

CATALOGING-IN-PUBLICATION DATA
Title: The town mouse and the country mouse.
Description: New York : Windmill Books, 2018. | Series: Let's learn Aesop's fables
Identifiers: ISBN 9781499483758 (pbk.) | ISBN 9781499483703 (library bound) | ISBN 9781499483604 (6 pack)
Subjects: LCSH: Fables. | Folklore.
Classification: LCC PZ8.2.A254 Tow 2018 | DDC 398.2--dc23

Manufactured in China.
CPSIA Compliance Information: Batch BS17WM: For Further Information contact Rosen Publishing, New York, New York at 1-800-237-9932

A little mouse who lived in a **busy, bustling town** was on a train to the country. He was going to visit his cousin. The town mouse was excited, as he had never been to the **country** before.

2

WELCOME

Meanwhile, the country mouse was hard at work preparing for the town mouse's visit.

3

After a long journey, the town mouse arrived. The cousins greeted each other joyfully.

"Hello!"

The country mouse showed off her home in a tree trunk. It was simple, but warm and cozy. "It doesn't look much like my home," the town mouse said.

Once the town mouse had rested, the country mouse took him to meet the farm animals next door. They crowded around to greet him.

6

Curious, the horse lowered his head and sniffed at the town mouse. "Watch it!" he cried. He wasn't sure about these new animals.

7

That evening, the country mouse served a dinner of bread and cheese. It was not at all like the fancy meals the town mouse was used to.

All night, the town mouse tossed
and turned in his bed of leaves.

He was used to sleeping
in a much softer bed.

9

"How do you put up with this?"
the town mouse asked in
the morning. "Your food is
plain and you sleep on leaves!"

10

"Come to the town with me and I'll show you how to live."

The country mouse was eager to see the town, so she agreed.

11

The town mouse lived in a giant house in the middle of town. The country mouse was amazed.

Inside, the town mouse proudly showed off his home. It was very **comfortable.**

The town mouse began a tour of the house. In the kitchen, they spotted a cat prowling around.

"Hide!" the town mouse whispered.

"Shhhhh!"

They scurried under a cup. Here they waited, hardly daring to breathe.

14

At last, the cat stalked away.
"That was close!" exclaimed
the country mouse, trembling.

15

Next, they crept into the living room. There were people there, watching a bright, glowing screen. The country mouse gazed at it —

she had never seen anything like it!

In the playroom, there were all kinds of toys. The country mouse knocked over a tower of building blocks, which came tumbling down.

Crash!

17

They then went to the dining room.
On the table, they found a
delicious-looking feast.

There were sandwiches and pies, cakes and cookies — everything that was good to eat. The mice helped themselves.

19

"I've never had food like this before!" said the country mouse. The town mouse laughed. "This is how you could eat all the time!" he replied.

"Yummy!"

20

Suddenly, the mice heard growling and scratching at the door.

Two dogs burst in, sniffing the air.

21

The dogs began to bark,
jumping up at the table.

The mice scampered away in fear.

Enough was enough.
The country mouse said goodbye
and left the town at once.

"Goodbye!"

"Better to live simply
in peace than richly
in fear," she said.